# POLARIS

## BY GAVIN MITCHELL

For Hornblower, Aubrey, Maturin, Bolitho (Richard and Adam) Biggles, Mackenzie, Cattermole, Woolley, Silk, Pearce, Severian, Captain Chris of Jersey, Sir Richard Grenville and all the others who know the freedom of the sea, the sky, the road and the land of fiction. In our current world without oceans, air or safe passage, all but one of those freedoms are very, very far away.

# 1.

'Captain O'Brian sends his compliments, and would Mr Midshipman Reeman please attend him at his earliest convenience.'

Ennis of the cutter's young gentlemen had uttered this in a piping treble; Reeman thought he was eleven if he was a day and knew even less of adolescence than he did of the sea. Reeman merely nodded and made his way to the captain's private chamber. Aboard a cutter privacy was a luxury and certainly unknown to the midshipmen, the young gentlemen, the other ranks, even the officers; and yet it was said that the warlock somehow had his own private chamber as well.

*The warlock.* Reeman shivered.

The captain looked up from his inevitable raft of paperwork and nodded. 'Ah, Reeman. Thanks for coming so promptly.' Reeman nodded gravely and fought to keep any irony from his expression; the very idea of a captain of a King's ship issuing a request which could be answered at the recipient's leisure was ludicrous, laughable.

'Just to put you at ease,' O'Brian continued, 'I've been trying to see everyone individually, within reason. I know this is an unusual situation-'

*That is putting it mildly,* Reeman thought.

'So I thought I might be able to resolve any issues, concerns, questions people might have.'

Reeman hesitated, confused, swaying not only with the inevitable motion of the vessel (compared to the huge line of battle ships on which he had mostly served for nearly half his life the cutter was like a thing alive) but also with bafflement at this new wrinkle to the situation. All previous captains in the King's navy that he had encountered were remote, distant figures of authority; on a ship weeks or even months from land they were one step close to God himself. This captain was more like someone's friendly uncle. And he was a captain full and post, with both epaulettes indicating his seniority even had his mass of grey hair not done so. In fact O'Brian was old even for his elevated rank; one of his advanced age would usually either be enjoying flag status or nursing considerable resentment. Yet there was no hint of resentment in his manner, nor in the amicable way he was conducting this apparent interview.

'Well, sir, it's like this.' Reeman began. 'I know it's not my place to question-'

'Say whatever you wish,' O'Brian smiled. 'It's only you and me here.'

Reeman could only consider the fresh irony that nothing on a King's ship was ever really confidential either; given how closely everyone was confined it was impossible to avoid overhearing conversations, to say nothing of the tendency of sailors to gossip to while away the long watches. Only the constant background noise of creaking timbers and ropes and men constantly at work above could possibly mask voices, and with the sea relatively calm today even that was low. 'Thank you sir. Well, it's like this.

I know this cutter is nearly new, experimental even, but there seems an abundance of officers and prime seamen. I thought a cutter would only ever be commanded by a lieutenant, but there's yourself, two commanders, three lieutenants, Kent and myself, five young gentlemen, not to mention all the warrant officers and prime seamen and topmen. I mean most King's ships are perpetually short handed and have to make up the shortfall in pressed landsmen who are more harm than good. I didn't even think a commander and a captain would be on the same ship!'

'Not a ship, Reeman, but you're right, they wouldn't in the normal course of events.'

'And yet we have maybe the finest crew in the King's navy. Most ships would give half their supplies to have even a few of our able seamen and we have been allocated them all. Surely they're needed to fight Bonaparte instead of helping us sail to... where, exactly?'

'Ah, now at this point I must chastise you, young Reeman,' O'Brian admonishing gently. 'You should know better than to ask to where we proceed. And it is always proceed, never sail or move...' O'Brian trailed away, staring into what was apparently the distance though the chamber was barely big enough for them both to fit into, and Reeman tried not to frown, wondering what he was staring at. Was the captain that easily prone to reverie?

'As you continue in your naval career,' O'Brian had snapped back to reality, 'you will learn that there are some questions that it is better not to ask.'

'Yes, sir.' Reeman swallowed. Even with this mild chastisement there was on issue burning a hole in his mind. 'But sir... permission to speak freely?'

'You may speak.' O'Brian offered a tired smile. 'Though whether I will respond to your liking is quite another matter.'

'This Mr Nemo...' said Reeman hesitantly. 'Is it true he's a warlock?'

The captain's smile was replaced with a frown, and he signed heavily. 'As I was saying, Reeman, there are some questions that it is better not to ask.'

The interview was over.

Later, Reeman and Kent were leaning on the larboard rail, staring out to sea and conversing in very low tones. A cutter was not so very large that a conversation could take place anywhere on deck and go unheard everywhere else, even in the rigging. However, with Commander Forester instructing the five King's letter boys in the fine art of determining position in the bow, the two midshipmen felt they could converse in relative privacy.

'He spoke to you too?'

'Indeed so,' Kent murmured. 'It sounds like virtually the same speech, the same questions. Everyone on board probably thought to ask why our company is so high-ranked. You were bold to ask where we were going, though.'

'I did of course ask the even bolder question,' Reeman muttered.

'Yes, I thought better of saying that myself. I did think of one reason why we might have so many officers on board. It's because-'

'Am I correct in thinking both of you just recently passed your examinations for lieutenant?'

A stern cold voice had snapped loudly behind them and made both boys flinch and jump. They spun round as one. Confronting them was Commander Robinson.

Robinson was nearly as old as the captain which made him of even more advanced age for his rank, his hair also grey but far more close-cropped; it was a long step from commander to captain, and many never made it. This might possibly explain his current freezing, hostile expression, but it was far more likely because, as Reeman realised with a sinking heart, they had both been caught genuinely in the wrong.

'Yes, sir,' answered both boys, the words partially overlapping.

'Had your Boards seen you both leaning on the rail passing the time of day, you would have both been failed, and rightly so.' Robinson's voice was pitched very loud, deliberately drowning out Forester's lecture on determining longitude. The other, younger commander had turned with a look of irritation, but quickly wiped it away to stare at Reeman and Kent with similar sternness. The young gentlemen with him could only gape. 'Had you considered what example you were setting to these children, to these men?' The men – all prime seamen and warrant officers – were generally hiding smirks as they studiously made a pretence of ignoring the Commander while deliberately making an appearance of going about their business. 'In forcing me to chastise you you have caused me to interrupt Commander Forester's lesson. So you have upset two King's officers of Commander rank and disrupted these King's letter boys' education and careers.'

'Sorry, sir,' both midshipmen said, realising the extent to which they were being made an example of.

'Get back to your tasks. And if you have none and cannot find something productive to do aboard a man of war at sea, God help you and your chances of promotion. Merely passing your Boards will *not* make you lieutenants, not until you are invited to take such a place on a King's vessel; and you will not earn the reputation that will get you asked this way. And God help the rest of us when foul weather comes or the enemy attacks if our supposed best and brightest think the correct use of their time is conversing idly.' Robinson abruptly spun on his heel and stalked away aft.

'Well, that was a bollocking and a half,' muttered Kent.

Humiliation was not to end there for the two passed midshipmen though. 'Since you have both been responsible for disrupting my lesson,' rang out the voice of Commander Forester, 'you may as well *continue* it. Come here and share with your younger peers the knowledge of navigation which let you pass the Board *despite* your constitutional idleness!'

Reeman's heart sank as the two of them plodded over to the group. The young gentlemen stared at them, all huge eyes and ill-fitting clothing. Commander Forester was grinning. Reeman stared at his new audience, totally frozen, his tongue cloven to the roof of his mouth, his lips glued together, unable to begin and not knowing how to, when-

'Hello, young sailors! Welcome to your navigation lesson! Your first question – can anyone tell me what this is?'

Kent had taken on an entirely new personality, somewhere between circus showman and enthusiastic parson. He produced a sextant from his coat with a flourish and brandished it.

'A sextant!' trilled a couple of the King's letter boys. Ostrander's voice broke half way through, and he gulped in embarrassment. Kent allowed him no time for self consciousness.

'Well done, young sailors! Now who can tell me what it is used for?'

Reeman was amazed at how much Kent was in his element with this, Reeman himself had every dread of crashing and burning. Perhaps that was the difference between himself and those who chose to tread the boards, that they were energised when they took it on and it put them outside of themselves. Reeman doubted he could ever have that power, and felt a moment's sadness... and jealousy.

'Can anyone tell me how it is used? Please supply instructions, and my assistant will follow them.'

Reeman had the sextant unceremoniously thrust into his hands. As the young gentlemen shrilled out orders, many of which would damage the instrument, he applied only those which wouldn't, reflecting on what an expensive device it was and ruefully thinking how sensible Kent had been not to actually give the younger boys the sextant to break themselves. As he manipulated the brass arms along the arc Reeman thought bitterly how he had never owned anything like this, and how his prime memory of being a young gentleman himself (apart from uninvited homosexual advances) was having his possessions stolen. Meanwhile Kent seemed born into this role, like a jester in permanent motley, and Commander Forester was watching him with eyebrows raised and an impressed expression. Even Commander Robinson had wandered back from aft and was watching intently, his cold, hostile expression now seeming like a mask of an assumed leadership role.

'That's it for the sextant, then. But now then, boys, who can tell me what *this* is?'

Kent took out an enormously elaborate brass disc of multiple layers, each with precisely shaped cutouts and minuscule etchings. The sunlight glinted off several jewels set into what appeared to be gold and silver filigree. The boys all stood dumb, mouths gaping open. Even the commanders looked overawed.

'This is an *astrolabe*, an Arabic instrument of great rarity and value. Even my assistant doesn't get to play with this.' The boys all giggled, Forester smiled, and Reeman ground his teeth and had the sudden urge to throw Kent's sextant into the briny deep. 'It was crafted by Musselmen using their unparalleled knowledge of mathematics and the stars.'

'Ah, the Musselman,' boomed a new voice on the ship, unfamiliar to Reeman. It was great, deep, timbrous and commanding, sounding more the part than even any of the senior offices. 'A religion of great nobility, but not yet entirely free of savagery.'

Reeman turned in curiosity to see who this speech belonged to and his blood ran icewater in his veins. It was the warlock. His great fat face, head and shoulders above many on board, was instantly recognisable, along with his disgustingly obscene totally shaved head which he did not cover decently with either wig or hat. But it was not this that struck

Reeman with total shock, or caused the boys to gape or even the commanders' eyes to open wide.

The warlock was bollock naked.

It was not even remotely warm on board, there was a biting wind as they headed almost directly north. The warlock did not seem at all disconcerted by this or even slightly cold. Not even his hairs were standing on end – and there was plenty of hair to see even despite the shaved head, Reeman observed dismally – and fought to tear his eyes away. Neither he nor even the young gentlemen, many of whom were having their first sea voyage, could be any stranger to the naked male form on a man of war. But the warlock's nudity was somehow uniquely abhorrent for no reason that could be defined – he was certainly both powerfully built and overweight, but there was no deformity or missing appendage visible.

Reeman did not know where to look. It was clear the King's letter boys and the two Commanders didn't know where to look either. Only Kent stared openly at the warlock, clearly fascinated. At least he was looking him full in the face rather than anywhere any lower down.

'I see you are wondering how I am able to appear on deck entirely unclothed in what must be admitted is inclement weather,' boomed the naked man. 'Long ago Iskander the Destroyer encountered what he called the naked philosophers when he entered the land of the Hindoos, who went unclothed out of ideological decision. The Indian lands are of course much warmer than here, but in both cases we owe our harditude to the practice of the ancient Hindoo art of *yoga*, taught to me by their holy fakir men on my travels there. Using these enlightened disciplines one becomes master of one's own body temperature despite the most hostile surroundings. I invite anyone to step forward and feel my hands, they will find them to be as warm as toast.'

Reeman couldn't imagine anything more horrible. The young gentlemen visibly cringed away, the Commanders looked as though they were inclined to do the same. Only Kent stepped forward; Reeman stared at him incredulously. The warlock offered his chubby paw and Kent took it curiously.

'You *are* warm,' the passed midshipman commented, grasping the hand and arm more firmly.

'Indeed so,' the nude man rumbled. 'I would be happy to share this knowledge with anyone who would be willing to study. Would you care to learn this power, young King's man?'

'Very much!' gasped Kent.

So matters stood on His Majesty's cutter, unrated vessel the *Polaris,* as the war against Napoleon raged on.

2.

'You should try that yoga Reeman, it's jolly useful.'

'No thanks,' the midshipman muttered. 'And don't let Robinson catch us talking again, it was bad enough last time.'

'Oh I won't,' Kent said, and pointedly moved to another part of the vessel.

The *Polaris* was anchored off the Scottish island of Skye, where the ship's surgeon, Mr Wolfe, had requested a stop over to study the sea eagles who nested there. Rather incredibly the Captain had granted this request. Even more incredibly, the warlock had gone with him, mercifully clothed in sensible attire this time. Though what was most incredible of all, in Reeman's experience, was for a ship's surgeon to take any interest in anything other than a bottle of strong drink. They were drunken butchers to a man, and Reeman prayed to Almighty God that he would never have any need of their services; though he knew full well the odds were that he would, and end up losing limbs, eyes or worse in the service of the King's navy.

However, it was by now widely known that Mr Wolfe was far more than the barely-trained amateurs the Navy sent to practice their questionable mercies on its jack tars. He was said to be a full physician, one of the most respected in the profession, member of learned societies, and allegedly would not get out of bed for less than ten guineas. He was out of bed now of course and for no money at all, braving the dangerous seas for nothing more than looking at some birds who no doubt did nothing but squawk, eat fish and cover the entire island with shit – and probably the ship as well, Reeman thought ruefully, knowing who would get the job of cleaning *that* up. Lieutenant Fullerton had taken Nemo and Wolfe over with a boat crew, and now the physician and the warlock were tramping over the island to their hearts' content.

'Deck there!' came the cry at the masthead.

As one the assembled men on the deck, working on their various tasks or pretending to, turned their attention to the yell. 'Sail to the west'rd!'

Captain O'Brian cursed, and clapped his telescope to his eye. 'Masthead there,' he yelled while scouring the sea, with the iron lungs of any seasoned naval officer, 'what manner of ship do you make it?'

'Brig, sir! Think it's French!'

O'Brian said an even worse oath, and snapped his telescope shut and to his side in frustration. 'Some of these prime seamen have superb eyesight,' he muttered, 'and knowledge too. Though this is of course not what we want to hear. Reeman, take this, go aloft and see if you can confirm.'

'Aye, sir.' Reeman took the captain's telescope – a superb, if unornate model – and scrambled up the rigging, thanking his lucky stars he had always been good at this, and never had any fear of heights.

He met the seaman at the masthead and greeted him gravely. The man was clearly a seasoned veteran, and relatively young; not one to make mistakes. Unfortunately.

'Over there, sir, can just make it out.'

Reeman looked, his heart sinking. The two masts were clear, and they had the weather gauge of the *Polaris* and were bearing down rapidly. It was impossible to see any flag at this distance, but many experienced seamen could indeed tell the nationality of vessels from their masts, rigging, sailplan, hull, or a myriad of other details.

He scrambled back down and returned the telescope. 'He's right sir. Coming down fast.'

'Deck there!'

This hail came from below, over the side of the ship in fact. Captain O'Brian looked over the rail and noted with surprise that Lieutenant Fullerton and the boat crew had gotten back from Skye already;

everyone must have scrambled aboard and they had made all speed rowing while Reeman was still climbing up and down. Standing in the sheets were the physician, and the warlock.

'Captain, you must run up the French colours!' called Mr Wolfe, his hands cupped around his mouth.

Reeman fought the urge to gasp. Who was the surgeon to give the Captain orders?

The captain frowned, pursing his lips. He stared again at the approaching vessel and then again at the surgeon. Then, unbelievably, he nodded. 'Mr Midshipman Simone, make it so.' The young gentleman, the expression of shock clear upon his face, scrambled to bend on the appropriate flag. For someone who had only learned this yesterday he did a fine job. The flag ran up the mast and burst into life.

Reeman felt a plucking at his sleeve. 'Mr Reeman, sir?' It was Mills, another of the King's letter boys.

'Yes, what is it?'

'Surely we're not allowed to run up the enemy's colours, sir?'

Reeman could only smile at the naiveté of the child's phrasing, though it was admittedly fair comment. 'Sailing, or approaching another vessel under false colours, or using them at this stage is counted as an acceptable ruse of war,' he explained gently. 'Fighting under false colours would be considered not.' Though he did not add that neither this nor anything else would surprise him at this stage.

By this point the boat crew, Nemo, Wolfe and Fullerton were scrambling back aboard. None needed a bosun's chair, though Wolfe was awkward as might have been expected of a civilian. The warlock, however, was quicker than the lieutenant and many of the prime seamen. Reeman had heard Nemo climbed mountains for his own amusement, though he had heard entirely too much of Kent's praise of what his fellow midshipman now insisted on calling 'the *magician*' and was getting rather tired of it.

The surgeon, though... Reeman stared at him as surreptitiously as he was able. He was an odd looking man, completely bald and again spurning the decent covering of a wig (though unlike the warlock he was clearly bald with old age; he was older even than the ship's officers, who were themselves all very aged for their rank) while sporting an enormous handlebar moustache that stretched from ear to ear and made him look like a walrus, creatures Reeman had seen occasionally in his long served apprenticeship for lieutenant.

The surgeon approached the captain, red faced and panting. 'Captain O'Brian, you must find all the men on this vessel who can speak French fluently,' he said, short of breath. 'Myself and Mr Nemo will then take them in this boat and approach the brig.'

Who was this man, again, to command a post captain of the King's navy?

O'Brian frowned, and shifted his gaze; but, incredibly, he did not turn to one of his own officers, but unbelievably, to the warlock. 'Myself and Mr Wolfe have conferred,' said the "magician" in tones that were, for him, astonishingly quiet and free from pomposity. 'This is the only possible solution.'

The captain stared out to sea. Reeman momentarily fancied he could hear him grinding his teeth. 'Lieutenant Johns, find all men who can speak French on board,' he snapped. 'And do it quickly, damn your eyes.'

Cursing the lieutenant was quite unnecessary; Reeman could only imagine how unwelcome being given orders from civilians was for O'Brian. In the circumstances, he was keeping a cool head.

Many men were found who could speak French, more than could actually fit in the boat. This was a function of the entire *Polaris* crew being elite material, of course, but also because Reeman had by now also noticed that the cutter was quite overmanned. It was difficult for him to consistently find tasks for everyone to do, particularly as they were all performed competently, quickly and enthusiastically; itself a rarity when so many men were pressed and so many more were incompetent or disabled. He had been on ships where practically all the deck jobs were carried out by men with ruptured bellies while everyone else was sent aloft to tend the sails and rigging. Nemo and Wolfe carried out their own weeding out of the candidates, barking French phrases at them and rejecting those who couldn't answer to their satisfaction. Lieutenant Donachie spoke French through long family connections; he passed the civilians' muster. He was along among the officers in knowing the language however. Still, eventually a full boat's crew was assembled. Reeman was not part of it; speaking French was not a skill he possessed, or had ever had the wherewithal to learn. Still, in a day full of surprises, another was yet to come.

Kent stepped forward. 'I speak French, magister.' Reeman frowned. Where was that from?

The warlock scowled at him, no longer being his special friend as the other passed midshipman made out. 'Quelle est la putain de langue que tu m'utilises?' Nemo barked.

'Le langage de nos nobles ennemis, maître,' Kent said smoothly.

The warlock frowned. 'All right, you'll do. Captain O'Brian, see that every man is armed with two pistols and a bladed weapon, all of which must be concealed within their clothing.'

Reeman's eyes went wide; he fought to keep the surgeon and warlock from noticing. This could not be the battle tactics of a gentleman. However, did this really matter in this case? Any brig was easily twice as powerfully armed as any cutter and easily held twice as many fighting men, even with the *Polaris* being overmanned with elite sailors and the possibility that their unknown adversary was under strength. Even a vessel with a skeleton crew only needed to man and fight one side's compliment of cannons, which was more than enough to blow

*Polaris* out of the water, while the cutter had little chance of causing much damage to the brig.

In any case though, the requisite quantity of pistols – of which the cutter had very many more than enough – were hurriedly loaded and primed and the bladed weapons prepared. All the men were for once decently clothed in better than adequate attire from the slop chest (Reeman had been on vessels where the captains were so uncaring of their men's wellbeing that the clothing the men had been pressed in was all they had and was allowed to fall to rags, leaving them naked or nearly so, with no opportunity provided to obtain more) and with a little ingenuity concealing the armament on every man was expedited. Conversely, none of the men had any clothing that might identify them as a Jack Tar of a King's vessel – Reeman had served on *other* ships where the captains, at their own personal expense and immense cost, had equipped their picked boatmen or even the entire crew with personalised uniforms.

Reeman began to have a sinking idea of how this was going to play out, and didn't like it at all.

With all the men armed with concealed weapons and crowded aboard the boat, it set off towards the French brig (by now its flag was clearly visible) in a choppy if navigable sea. The surgeon was crouched down hanging on for dear life, clearly not a man who had yet got his sea legs (and might never do so) but the warlock stood erect, leaning on one knee dramatically, the other hand holding a stout walking stick planted vertically into the planks of the boat as though he might drive it through. Reeman watched the boat shrinking away into the distance with heavy heart. Was this what the British navy, which he had served all his life and never wanted anything else, was coming to?

The boat was a long time reaching the brig and a still longer time elapsed after everyone had scrambled aboard, the tiny figures just visible. Occasionally men would pick up telescopes and stare at it, though Captain O'Brian never did, merely staring at the brig with unhappy mouth and watery eyes which could only have been caused by the wind and glare. Time passed, and passed, and passed. Eventually everyone got bored of their telescopes and they all just stared. But, for all the many long minutes that elapsed since the world had changed for everyone aboard the *Polaris,* it somehow surprised nobody when the French colours on the brig were hauled down and the King's colours hauled up in their place.

3.

'And then the surgeon stabbed the French captain and it was *beautiful!*

The gun room had always been the traditional domain of midshipmen, even though on the cutter there was scarcely room for them all. Over their plentiful supply of alcohol and uncharacteristically abundant supply of food Kent was regaling the King's letter boys with tales of his adventures aboard the brig, on which the *Polaris* crew had carried the day with little loss of life but appallingly dishonourable tactics. The younger boys were all staring at Kent in rapt awe and worship; Reeman was grinding his teeth with rage.

'Mr Midshipman Aaron, pass me that wine again, if you please. Awfully nice of your father to give you this, a marvellous vintage. He wanted you to give it to the captain? Well I'm sure O'Brian has plenty of his own drinks and to spare, it won't be wasted here with us! Cheers!' Kent crowed to the young gentlemen's delight and the other passed midshipman's disgust and growing hatred.

As Reeman had expected, the boat had made its way towards the French brig (now known to be called the *Voltaire*) while expecting Napoleon's sailors and troops to believe they were their countrymen. This was of course a story that was scarcely believable and hardly one that could never have been tried before, and the *Polaris's* men had found themselves confronted with an armed guard only one step away from actually aiming their muskets at them and a deeply suspicious commander and complement of officers.

However, the surgeon and the warlock had hailed the *Voltaire* in flawless French, and from this point on the story had inspired, and continued to inspire, Reeman with growing anger. Wolfe had convinced the enemy that he was one of Napoleon's top physicians and Nemo was his scholarly adjutant, and together they were touring the tyrant's vessels, surveying the state of the men and helping out where they could. This would again have been a tale hardly credible except that the warlock transpired to have a disturbing ability to make men believe whatever he wished... because after all, however else would he have come by his reputation, his appellation?

'His most basic technique,' slurred Kent in a stage whisper, now heavily intoxicated, 'is to look at people but instead he's focussed his eyes on a point beyond them. See?' He demonstrated it on Reeman at the other end of the table, who found the vacant gaze (already made stupid with drink) merely made him more infuriated. 'It's like you're looking through people, and-'

Whatever the efficacy of this stare or Kent's rendition of it the surgeon and the warlock had somehow wholly convinced the Frenchmen that their story was true, and the entire crew of the boat was soon taken aboard and into the confidence of the enemy. Wolfe had offered his services to the captain, Nemo had gone to speak with the chaplain, Lieutenant Donachie had been welcomed to the French wardroom and the men had joined their

new drinking partners for alcohol and tall tales...
but at the most perfect moment, each of the
Englishmen had stabbed or shot the most
opportune target and the shock and surprise had
carried the day. In most cases the wounds had not
even been lethal. The crew of the brig had
surrendered, the majority had been pressed into
service more willingly than not (it seemed
Napoleon's perfect republic of liberty, fraternity and
equality was not all it had been sold to them as)
and those few who would not cooperate had been
taken prisoner. The men of the *Polaris* now
commanded two vessels, a powerful brig not the
least puissant amongst them.

'And that's why we now have another playground,
and more drink! Huzzah!' Kent's huzzah was echoed
by the King's letter boys, many of whose voices
were breaking or not yet broken.

'And the tactics of a pack of blackguards!' Reeman
shouted over the table.

The young gentlemen went quiet and sat in silent anxiety. Kent stared back at his opposite number, inebriated and truculent.

'I advise you to be more careful what you say, sir,' he slurred, taking another pull at Aaron's father's wine.

'I am indeed careful what I say and what I do. I have always striven to comport myself as an officer and a gentleman, something that seems not to bother you, Mr Kent. Perhaps any of you King's letter boys can tell me what the French and Spanish navies will start doing if it becomes known that the British behave in this way?'

There was an intense, uncomfortable silence. None of the younger teenagers would meet his gaze; Kent merely glowered.

'At best they will start using those tactics themselves. At worst they will start treating each and every Jack Tar as a suitable target for revenge for this day's work. This is a civilised age, in which prisoners of war are entitled to expect and receive humane treatment. What do you think will happen to British prisoners if the British become known for dishonourable behaviour? We will be treated worse than common pirates. Compared to some of the possible fates – particularly to boys – the noose would seem a blessing.'

'The only honour in war is winning,' hissed Kent. His lack of slurring of this phrase at this point merely indicated it was a common refrain to him.

'I do not appreciate your views, sir, or the example you are setting here. You may have passed to become a King's officer, but you are no gentleman.'

Kent hurled his glass to the side; it shattered, a highly irresponsible act in an environment where most of the common sailors went barefoot. 'I do not like your words or your tone sir! I demand satisfaction!'

'You demand, and you will get-'

'THERE WILL BE NO SATISFACTION DEMANDED ABOARD THIS VESSEL!'

Captain O'Brian burst into the gunroom, his face like thunder. In the past Reeman had seen captains who were clearly feigning anger to chastise men. This anger was clearly unfeigned. In the cramped gunroom the senior officer was a huge, physical presence; Reeman cringed involuntarily, thinking for one moment the captain meant to tear him from his seat and beat him with his fists.

'Foolish children, you can be heard! Have you forgotten the size of a cutter? Your stupidity is clearly audible to the ends of the bowsprit and masthead. Though such talk is unacceptable aboard any size of King's vessel. By rights you should both be flogged. Reeman, Kent, you are denied strong drink for a month, and anyone who sneaks any to you shall themselves be denied drink for two months. I shall personally see to it that you both get every shitty job going until such time as I judge you suitably punished. And you shall be separated. Mr Midshipman Reeman, you are hereby transferred to the *Voltaire*, effective immediately. Get your sea chest and leave. And I'll take that wine. Mr Aaron, my compliments to your father.' Giving them one final, disgusted glance, the captain made his exit.

This time there was no comradely joke between the two passed midshipmen. Reeman stood, turned on his heel, and walked out to get his belongings without a word.

# 4.

Rapidly into the course of his exile aboard the *Voltaire* many things became clear to Reeman, though not all at once but one after another. The first which struck him immediately was that he was indeed saddled with every shitty job going – and there were many, many shitty jobs to be done aboard any blue water vessel. Reeman was of course aware of all of these from his long served apprenticeship to lieutenant rank, and had performed most of them. The difference was that previously they had arisen out of the course of his duties, or an impartial rota – for someone whose entire goal all his life had been to become a King's officer and who had always strived never to put a foot wrong, even in the face of all the temptations available, being put on punishment detail was a bitter, intolerable hurt.

Reeman had known midshipmen who had smuggled girls aboard and kept them for the entire durations of voyages, midshipmen who ruthlessly bullied and abused, even raped, the common seamen to satisfy some twisted lust for power, and midshipmen who gleefully engaged in gambling on a scale that would get the men flogged clear down to the spine. Now he thought about it he remembered rumours that Kent was particularly infamous for this last; his mouth twisted, remembering that priceless astrolabe. However Reeman had never done any of this and took pride in never having done anything else wrong. To someone with a spotless copybook having this enormous black mark against him and to have to work it out publicly in sight of everyone was an almost physical agony; no doubt this was precisely what the captain had intended.

And yet as time went on Reeman was forced to conclude that there were ulterior motives for O'Brian's decision as well. Lieutenant Donachie had stayed aboard the *Voltaire* and taken command as the only officer able to speak French – though Reeman noted with bitter irony that this was the first time on this mission someone with appropriate rank was commanding the appropriate rating of vessel. The Frenchmen and Englishmen had been divided amongst the vessels and mixed about as much as possible so as to minimise the likelihood of the French abruptly mounting a rebellion, though they seemed to work with their new crewmates happily enough. Meanwhile however, the surgeon and the warlock had immediately decided that only the largest vessel available was good enough for them and promptly had all their accoutrements moved to new private rooms aboard the brig. Reeman slowly realised that this meant two things.

The first was that Kent was still confined aboard the cutter undergoing his own punishment duties, and while – unlike Reeman – this didn't seem to bother him, it did mean he was effectively separated from the warlock, with whom he had been spending entirely too much time and listening to and learning Christ alone knew what. Reeman could only conclude this was deliberate on the part of the captain also, and thought it an entirely admirable and necessary decision.

The second however was that the warlock was now on a different ship to O'Brian – who was notably not exercising his right as post captain to command the largest vessel – and Reeman rapidly began to realise that this must have been a deliberate decision on the part of Captain O'Brian as well, on the grounds that he had had an entire gutful of the warlock and his shit. Reeman was also forced to conclude that being stuck aboard the same vessel as the self-styled magician was an additional part of his punishment for, whatever magical powers he might or might not possess, he was an entirely pompous, unsufferably pretentious ass.

'Mr Nemo, sir-' he had approached the warlock on deck one day.

'My name is not Nemo!' the great fat face had boomed, drowning out even the leather-lunged bosuns and masters' mates calling out orders on how to set the rigging. 'Nemo is merely what I became after I passed the Abyss, when I was stripped of all my accomplishments and of myself as well. Before I was hacked apart by Choronzon and became a Babe of the Abyss I was known as Marten Broadcloak, Randall Flagg, Walter O'Dim,

Frater Perdurabo, Hugo Rune and once, even, Edward Alexander. But that man is dead. I have crossed the Abyss and awakened the Kundalini seven times, and my Arete enlightenment level stands at 7.'

The man of many names and more annoyances paused expectantly. Reeman realised he was supposed to say something. 'So you're a warlock then,' the midshipman said sourly, feeling his alcohol ban particularly keenly at that moment.

The alleged witch's eyes had bulged in outrage, not a good look in a man so large, overweight and bald. 'I am no warlock!' he had howled, dressed at that time in a ridiculously elaborate robe, presumably of his own devising, with multiple layers of colour and massive winged collars. Surrounded by sailors in practical naval gear he looked ridiculous and not a little fruity. 'That word translates in Old English to oath breaker. I am a *magician*, and no magician would ever use the term. Warlock also implies evil intent, and the difference between white and black magick is that with one the intent is benign and with the other the intent is perverse. When one does not cross the Abyss but instead takes the Left-handed Path and becomes one of the Black Brotherhood-'

And so on and on, an endless stream of information of infinite pretentiousness, apparent nonsense and no interest or meaning whatever to Reeman. The warlock was constantly declaring, teaching, informing, as though he was the master of all knowledge and Reeman the poor bloody shit in the street. On Reeman's worst days the warlock, finding no one else to listen to him, would follow the midshipman on his punishment duties and just talk and talk and talk, never at low volume and completely indifferent to any of Reeman's responses or lack of them. Reeman could imagine no fresher hell.

Still, that was just the warlock. The surgeon was even worse.

On the face of it Mr Wolfe was affable and likeable enough, even charming in a wet kind of way. He was possessed with a boundless enthusiasm for absolutely everything which was initially entertaining but which rapidly grated. This was understandable enough when it concerned creatures like albatrosses – 'Oh, excellent!' Wolfe would gush after spying one of the vast-winged birds following the brig, no doubt hoping for food scraps. 'What beautiful, magnificent animals!' On this occasion Reeman was prepared to concede that an albatross was indeed a beautiful and magnificent animal (and made good eating, as he was able to testify from one rare incredible stroke of luck on one of his tours of duty aboard a man of war) and brought warmth to the cockles of his heart, possibly even the sub cockle area. However, the surgeon's *joie de vivre* extended to everything possible, including the totally mundane. 'What marvellous work!' he would exclaim after stepping past a crew of men swabbing the deck, who would subsequently stare after him incredulously. He also went into raptures when one of the master's mates caught a squid by desultorily dangling a fishing line over the side, and was more than happy to swap the squid with the master's mate for a large infusion of cash.

It might, indeed would, have been expected that such behaviour would cause the common seamen to view him with derision and sneer at him behind his back, possibly even to his face; but instead they were all in awe of the surgeon and thought he was great. Reeman could again understand this up to a point; it was unheard of for the normal naval surgeon to be in any way sober, qualified or competent, and from the normal calibre of the dregs foisted upon crews by the Admiralty one would think that any hint of medical merit was severely frowned upon. Compared with this Mr Wolfe seemed like God's holy gift.

However, as time went on Reeman began to have... concerns. No one had died in the engagement in which the *Polaris* had taken the brig; while there had been many stabbings and shootings Wolfe had managed to operate, remove any bullets or shrapnel and stitch any wounds after him. However, from his experience Reeman knew that wounds inflicted aboard a ship did not often heal cleanly (particularly when fragments of metal, wood, canvas and so on were carried into the body) and men falling victim to infection and gangrene was a distressing regularity. None of this happened here and everyone healed perfectly, even with minimal scarring. Either the surgeon had some heretofore unknown methods of disinfectant or aftercare, or there was something else operating here.

And the solution to one wound filled the rest of the crew with awe, but Reeman with horror.

A few of the Frenchmen had managed to get shots off during the *Polaris's* takedown, and one of the English crew had taken a musket shot from a muzzle that was virtually touching him. It had blown away a chunk of his left side taking his lower ribs (which Reeman had heard referred to as 'floating') with it, and the associated part of his lung. In Reeman's world up until now this would have been an automatic death sentence, but the surgeon had fixed it with aplomb. The solution was certainly practical and ingenious, but it seemed that it filled only Reeman with abject dread and disgust.

Wolfe had essentially riveted a piece of canvas to the seaman's side, simply covering the hole which still seemed to be empty of flesh and bone. Reeman could only assume Wolfe had cauterised the raw bleeding meet remaining after the musket ball carried the rest away, otherwise the man would have rapidly bled to death. Now, as the crew member breathed in and out, the canvas exhibited what Reeman had been taught was the paradoxical movement characteristic of flail chest, where a section of ribs through blunt trauma had become detached from the rest. Such that, when the man breathed out, as his chest fell the canvas bulged outwards, and when his shoulders rose as he inhaled the canvas sucked in.

The rivets were all clearly visible at the edge of the cleanly cut and shaped patch of sailcloth, and seemed driven through the flesh with cruel force, as the skin surrounding the canvas was red and inflamed, even laced with black threads which to

Reeman screamed of infection. All this was clearly visible because far from being horrified by his prosthetic side himself, the seaman was delighted by it and wore no shirt constantly so as to keep showing it off to his admiring companions. 'I'd of been a goner if not for that fine Mr Wolfe!' he would declaim to all and sundry, clear as a bell in a soft Bristol accent.

He wore no shirt despite the weather getting colder and colder, not least because of the shortening of the days with the season but also due to the fact that they were steadily heading north. The ultimate orders of the mission were of course secret, and Reeman as a passed midshipman no longer had the irksome busywork duty of taking the position of the ship every day with the young gentlemen and handing his results in to the captain, but their prevailing direction of travel would have been obvious to the smallest child, let alone an experience sea officer candidate.

But there was one aspect of the lung prosthetic which horrified Reeman the most, over and above its incredible nature and that by all rights the man should be dead. The entire surface of the sailcloth was closely covered with writing. There was the Latin alphabet, Reeman recognised Greek letters from his mandatory knowledge of trigonometry for his sailing studies, and he could also see the Hebrew letters used by the Jewish merchants on shore. But there were other alphabets and symbols he couldn't hope to identify, though he could see what he thought were the symbols for the planets which he'd heard were also associated with metals, and words he could read but which disturbed him immeasurably like TETRAGRAMMATON, SATOR AREPO, BELPHEGOR and worse phrases which crawled in his skin even though he couldn't understand them. He had heard the warlock pontificate about 'Enochian – the language of the angels' and he had no doubt about who had added all this writing to the canvas, before or after it was riveted in place.

*Witchcraft.* It made Reeman's blood run cold.

Thus matters stood on the paired vessels *Polaris* and *Voltaire,* as they headed ever northward.

# 5.

Time passed.

After three and a half weeks Reeman's alcohol ban was quietly forgotten about, though the midshipman was absolutely sure that nothing on King's vessels was ever 'quietly forgotten about' and it was vastly more likely that Captain O'Brian had taken pity on him and had his orders conveyed to the brig to let Reeman off, even though ostensibly the communications between the brig and the cutter were administrative only. Reeman could only hope that Kent had not been let off his alcohol ban in the same casual manner; after all, it was the other passed midshipman that had got them both into this mess, and Reeman had had ample time to reflect on this.

While his alcohol ban had been lifted and was of immeasurable comfort, the directive for the lieutenant candidate to get 'every shitty job going' had not. This however, seemed a necessity; like the cutter from the very start of the mission, the brig was very overmanned; and there was now the additional complication that more than half the brig's crew were impressed Frenchmen, most of whom spoke no English. While Lieutenant Donachie spoke fluent French he relied on Reeman and the other warrant officers for delegation, and since the French speaking crew members had been mixed between the brig and the cutter the fluent were few in number and the language barrier was frequently a problem. Fortunately the defectors were more than happy to teach Reeman their lingo which he took to with the ease of the young and eager.

The impressed Frenchmen were indeed more than pleased to serve their new masters aboard the *Voltaire* and the *Polaris*, and Reeman could only wonder if this was down to their disenchantment with Napoleon, their eagerness to be aboard an apparently successful mission as opposed to a sea war which was not in the tyrant's favour, their awe at the fantastic talents of the surgeon, or the supposed mental influence of the warlock. There remained of course those few Frenchmen who had refused to join the British, and these were kept under armed guard in the lowest levels of the brig, forbidden to all but the surgeon and the warlock. Sometimes screams and sobbing could be heard echoing through the vessel and some of the French, Irish or other Catholics would cross themselves, to be lampooned or lambasted by their companions. Given the sight of the canvas lung patch what might be being inflicted on the prisoners by Nemo and Wolfe was best not imagined.

Reeman himself was pleased with none of this, and as time went on he was increasingly disgusted with the author of his distress, the young man and supposed comrade who had provoked the outburst that had got him into this punishment exile; Mr Midshipman Kent, the dung. Now that he had had time to brood Reeman had thought of plenty of reason to dislike Kent from the start. Looking back his fellow passed midshipman was subject to constant drunkenness, not just on his daily allowance of grog but on supplies smuggled aboard by himself, cajoled, bargained or bullied from virtually everyone else short of the captain and commanders. He had heard tell of Kent's legendary gambling even before meeting the lad himself, and his flourishing of that priceless astrolabe had made such stories easy to believe, particularly as he had heard nothing of any special interest invested in Kent by anyone in the Navy, or of any very wealthy background possessed by the man. In the normal course of events these attributes and his confident, cocky manner might have been endearing to Reeman, made Kent seem like a 'character' and someone worth befriending, but having caused him weeks of misery they led to an undying hatred.

There was also the fact that Reeman suspected that part of the reason for the passed midshipmen's separate exile and punishment was to keep Kent away from the warlock. This had only been a partial success as every time there were dispatches carried between the British vessels in a jollyboat Mr Nemo had a packet for Kent – 'my eager young student' as the self-styled magician boasted to anyone who would listen. Satanic material for the wild boy to pore over and practice no doubt. It killed Reeman to think a once promising King's officer was being led along this forsaken path by the fat, disgusting witch.

Reeman was aware that such grudges had no place in the Navy. In the field of battle you could afford to have none but comrades standing beside you; and in the crowded living conditions aboard blue water vessels, in which you were stuck with the same few men for months and years, conversations over the dinner table or over shared work had to be kept convivial – maintaining them as such was the hallmark of most successful officers. He was also of the opinion that keeping such grudges was crude and base and immature, and he hated himself for it; but he could not persuade himself otherwise.

His thoughts were occupying this dismal circle once again as he stood on watch duty one freezing day in a cold damp fog. Reeman's eyes ached as he gazed into the grey nothingness, but he had no choice but to do it.

'Deck there!' came the call.

'Masthead!' shouted Reeman back. 'What do you see? Is there an end to this fog?'

'Frigate, sir!' One of the older hands, one of the hard men who took pride in working with a teeth-clenched cynicism which was very much of an act while he quietly assisted less experienced men with their duties, the lookout's voice was yet tinged with panic. 'Spanish colours!'

'Mother of God,' said a master's mate beside Reeman in a soft Dubliner lament.

And then they were out of the fog and into weak sunlight, the worst thing that could have happened at the worst time. To the larboard side was the *Polaris,* really too close than would have been wished in any weather; the helmsmen spun their wheels frantically to add distance. But bearing down on them fast, as threatened, was an awful sight.

Reeman clapped his telescope to his eye. At this distance the frigate was close enough to read the name *Cervantes,* and make out every detail of the figurehead, presumably the venerable man of letters himself. The Spanish man of war had the weather gauge of both British ships, and there was very little at this point could save them. Frigates were renowned for being faster than anything stronger and stronger than anything faster, and with three multi-sectioned masts crammed with sail, a brig or even a cutter would be hard pressed to outrun one even in the best of circumstances. Caught off guard with the wind in the Spaniard's favour, *Polaris* and *Voltaire* had little chance of doing anything at all.

Reeman's trained seaman's brain started running through options frantically. If the brig and the cutter scattered, made a break for it separately, there was a chance one of them could be saved. But which one? As one who aspired to be a King's officer his instinct was to save the post captain, but the Admiralty in their wisdom had clearly decided the surgeon and the warlock were at the centre of their mission, and-

'Captain O'Brian!' hollered the warlock between the vessels. At this distance it was possible to communicate with lung power. 'You must strike our colours.'

There was an intense, awful silence. Reeman stared at the warlock in disbelief, then at the stern deck of the cutter. Captain O'Brian was clearly visible, flanked by Forester, Robinson and half a dozen others. The midshipman could not make out their expressions but he had no doubt they were as incredulous as his own.

It was notable that O'Brian did not answer himself, though as Reeman had seen on innumerable occasions, like all post captains he was quite capable of making himself heard in all weathers. Instead he was seen to visibly and not gently prod a nearby young gentleman, who took up a speaking trumpet. 'Communication not clear,' came the distorted, broken voice of the child. 'Say again.'

'You must strike!' yelled the surgeon, who could shout nearly as loudly. Reeman stared in horror back and forth between the great fat face of the warlock, Wolfe and his walrus mustache, his senior officers on the other ship. The midshipman realised that Lieutenant Donachie was standing beside him, muttering to himself in what sounded like Scottish Gaelic. Reeman could only assume it was a prayer.

*They can't really do this... can they?*

Reeman had a sudden dreadful idea of how this situation might play out.

By now, the two British vessels not having done anything to save themselves, the frigate had advanced on them with blinding speed and was now close enough to read its name with the naked eye, count the Spaniards crowding the prow and watch the marksmen scrambling into place in the *Cervantes'* rigging and levelling their muskets at the Englishmen. The Spanish sailors were even taking in sail to slow the frigate's advance before there was a head on collision. Bow chasers were being set up pointing directly at Reeman and O'Brian, or so it seemed as he stared straight down the muzzle of one. No doubt they would be filled with canister and grapeshot to sweep the decks of the British vessels clean.

Reeman tore his gaze from the black hole into hell and stared across at the post captain. To his horror, O'Brian visibly hung his head, then made a gesture towards the centre of the vessel. A sword swung, and the King's colours came fluttering to the floor. The brig followed suit.

At this point Reeman's *best* hope was to be captured and spend the rest of the war languishing in a Spanish prison.

But it was all over now bar the formal protocols of surrender. Everyone knew the drill. The crew of the *Polaris* and the *Voltaire* stood on the decks empty handed, making no attempt to reach for any sort of weapon, as the Spaniards hurled grappling irons over their railings, to meet with no resistance. The British vessels were hauled to the frigate, lashed alongside and Spaniards came pouring aboard, armed to the teeth. Reeman found himself staring into the eyes of a frowning, moustached, middle aged Spanish warrant officer, holding a pistol and a cutlass pointed loosely at the sky. It was not belligerence with which he gazed at Reeman though, but puzzlement. Reeman could read his thoughts as easily as if they had been in English. *Why did you surrender?*

Reeman could only pray his worst fears would not yet be realised.

The Spanish sounded their own notes of ceremony, and their captain came aboard the brig. There was some puzzlement as he stared back and forth between Lieutenant Donachie and the post captain on the cutter. It was obvious that he had come aboard the bigger vessel expecting the higher ranking officer to be aboard, but this was clearly not the case. He visibly decided to cut his losses and proceed.

'Good afternoon, senor,' he said to Donachie. 'I am Don Fernando Lafuente y Clavero of His Most Catholic Majesty's Navy of Espana. I have the honour of receiving your surrender, and you have my word that yourself and your men will be treated fairly. As a demonstration of your good faith... your sword, please.'

Reeman could see agony on Donachie's face and almost sense it flowing through the air between them. His sword had every appearance of being a priceless family heirloom, passed down from generation to generation, perhaps even wielded by Donachie flag officers of the past. But Nemo and Wolfe had left him no choice.

Donachie drew his sword and gazed down at it, perhaps wanting to fix it in his memory for the last time. He started to turn his hilt to the Don.

It was at this moment that the warlock pulled a pistol of curious design from beneath his robes and shot the Spanish captain through the head.

'*Now* we fight,' he said, and all hell broke loose.

Reeman sobbed, his worst fears realised, but he had no choice now but to pull out his midshipman's dirk and stab the Spaniard opposite him in the throat. The man died with a look of confusion as much as betrayal. But then Reeman was fighting for his life.

As Reeman slashed aboat him at anyone he didn't recognise, first with his dirk and then with a cutlass snatched from a dying man in his other hand, he had little time to take in anything but the immediate threat, but a few things struck him in the fog of war. Nemo and Wolfe had one of the curious pistols in each hand and were blasting repeatedly; incredibly, without having to reload between shots. Reeman somehow caught sight of his hated rival Kent on the cutter; he too had a pair of the strange repeaters. But the biggest horror was Donachie, who had been prepared to surrender just seconds earlier, stabbing and slashing about him with his ancestral sword with a look of absolute joy and singing at the top of his voice in Scottish.

*Joy*? In this battle without honour? They were now lower than beasts, which lived without honour to begin with and could not be dishonoured. But the Englishmen had thrown it all away.

At the start of the battle the Spaniards had had every advantage. But the treacherous headshot had clearly shocked them to the core. This might have led them to fight with absolute fury butchering every man jack of the British, but the sight of the repeater pistols clearly horrified them while it inspired the English and their French converts to lunatic highs of violence. It was not long before the Spanish aboard the *Polaris* and the *Voltaire* were throwing down their weapons and crying for mercy, and the British sailors were swarming aboard the *Cervantes*. The fighting men who had been left there were appalled by the surrender of their comrades and swiftly followed suit. Nemo and Wolfe stalked aboard the captured frigate like conquering heroes to the cheers of the comrades; the convoy had gained another ship.

Reeman hurled his dirk and cutless to the deck. At that moment he no longer wanted to live in this world.

6.

But Reeman had to go on living. He also had to retrieve his dirk from where he had thrown it down.

Events followed the same predictable pattern as before. The frigate was taken over by the King's navy or those who now owed allegiance to them. The vast majority of Spaniards agreed to join the winning force, perhaps not realising in advance that in fact the majority were French defectors to the British crown by this point. These Spaniards were well distributed between the three vessels, though preventing them realising that original English navy men were in the minority was perhaps a lost cause at this point. It seemed not to cause any problem however. Either they were as disillusioned with the King of Spain as the Frenchmen had been with Napoleon, or in both cases, there was indeed something to the warlock's personal magnetism. Reeman had never seen it, and couldn't see it now.

He was occupied however with the new distribution of officers and the new administrative regime aboard the vessels. Forester was the more senior of the commanders and was given the frigate – though in stark defiance of the Naval tradition that a frigate was a post-captain's command. In the normal course of events, a mere commander would never be given such. Flying in the face of naval tradition again was Captain O'Brian's obstinate refusal to leave the original Navy cutter *Polaris* on which they had started the mission. O'Brian was still in nominal command of the whole enterprise, although it was sadly obvious who was really in charge. The warlock and the surgeon had of course immediately decamped for the frigate.

Also assigned to the *Cervantes* was Lieutenant Fullerton and three of the young gentlemen, all of whom had survived this far – a detail which perturbed Reeman. Once again, none of the crew of the *Voltaire* or the *Polaris* had died in the engagement (though many had lost limbs or sustained grievous wounds, all of which were still subject to the tender mercies of Mr Wolfe) and when crew members of the Cervantes actively and officially defected to the King's navy none of them died subsequently either – even though they too had often been badly hurt. This detail perturbed Reeman more and more.

*No one ever dies... what have we become?*

The passed midshipman found himself detailed to support Fullerton and Forester aboard the new frigate – and to his surpassing disgust, so was Kent. Reeman found himself assigned to mess in the wardroom of the *Cervantes* with Lieutenant Fullerton and Mr Midshipman Kent, even though the two younger men were still technically warrant officers; presumably, with Commander Forester having the private cabin that went with command, the Lieutenant felt he wanted the company. The young gentlemen were relegated to the gun room, presumably a very childish domicile with the lot of them not yet done with puberty.

Commander Forester proved himself to be extremely genial and very adept at maintaining polite and uncontroversial conversation, and Reeman followed suit, though it was notable that neither he nor Kent ever directly addressed each other. Kent was ostensibly pleasant himself, though he made frequent comments that could be taken as having two meanings (one always detrimental to Reeman) and Reeman often caught Kent staring at him with an insulting smirk. Reeman successfully kept down the urge to wipe it off the other midshipman's face.

By this point Reeman had been able to get a good look at one of the repeating pistols which had been used to such devastating effect in the battle to take the *Cervantes*. He had to admit the design was amazingly ingenious though he was appalled by a world that would soon call such things commonplace, especially when allied to the tactics used by the warlock and surgeon. Essentially, the rear part of the pistol was five short barrels welded together in a pentagon shape, such that they were all in parallel. There was just enough length of tube to insert a charge of gunpowder, a pistol ball and the wadding to hold them all in place. The pistol's owner repeated this exercise for each of the five small sections of barrel, there was then a single longer section of tube held by the weapon's framework in front of the wadding and ball. When the trigger was pulled, the welded sections were rotated by one fifth of a circle to bring a fresh charge behind the long barrel and the pistol's serpentine was automatically pulled back; when all were lined up, the hammer fell and the repeater fired its ball with a deafening report and a huge cloud of smoke. Even if there was a misfire on one charge another trigger pull would bring the next one forward.

The mechanism relied on the new-style percussion caps which were still very rare compared to the flintlock, and the pull on the trigger was so punishing that only the hardest of sailmakers could manage it without using two fingers. Still, the weapon was enormously powerful for the morale effect as much for the physical damage, and every blacksmith aboard the vessels was now hard at work churning out new repeaters, to Reeman's partial admiration but greater disgust.

And the convoy headed ever north, though they rarely caught sight of land any longer and knowing the exact position of the ship was not part of Reeman's duties. It was extremely cold and the passed midshipman had taken to requisitioning articles from the slop chest to wear actually under his uniform, though this was frequently difficult to conceal and made it quite a bit harder to move. Worryingly, in accordance with the pattern previously established none who had been treated by the surgeon since the taking of the *Cervantes* seemed to feel the cold; Kent, of course, actively flaunted his ability to resist the environment in all weathers despite that he had remained uninjured.

The increasing numbers of sailors sporting replacement limbs and disturbing injury grafts was also a concern to Reeman. Making the prosthetics look remotely human or mundane was clearly not a priority for the surgeon (and perhaps it was a point of pride not to). Wolfe also, in stark contrast with every other treatment Reeman had ever observed, favoured metal over wood. It was now common to see seamen with metallic limbs which looked more insectile than human and made Reeman feel queasy to look at them. Some of the prosthetic legs had hinged ankles or knees (which Reeman had seen before on particularly wealthy officers) but these seemed to have a freedom, even an *independence*, of movement which was unprecedented; those few the passed midshipman had previously encountered seemed to rely on crude springs.

Even worse were the hands and arms, which seemed capable of grasping rope or spars with no visible means of articulation and even allowed fine motion of the fingers, albeit with the wrong number, length or jointing of the fingers – the surgeon never made two pieces remotely alike, perhaps for the challenge. The seamen would brag and boast about their 'enhancements' whereas previously they might have declaimed of their sea battles or sexual conquests. Worst of all was Mills, of the young gentlemen, who tragically had had his young life cut short by having the top right hand third of his head, down to the eye and cheekbone, shot away. Or so it had seemed to begin with. Mills now had an entire section of his face and skull made of hammered bronze, complete with a glass eye in which smoke seemed to swirl. Sometimes Reeman felt he could discern the eye rotating in the socket and seeming to focus its gaze... And, needless to say, each prosthetic had its loading of dreadful runes and ungodly names, those few Reeman could decipher. The warlock had just a big a hand in their creation as Wolfe. Tortured screams, sobbing, and sounds of prayers in French, Spanish, even Gaelic, Dutch and other languages could still be heard from the forbidden zones where those who would not defect were held; Nemo and the surgeon evidently still felt the need to experiment.

After the addition of the frigate the convoy began to outright prey upon shipping. There was little that sailed the seas that could stand against a cutter, a brig and a frigate, all fighting together. Most merchants surrendered without a fight, to be overrun, their men pressed into service and their vessels added to the growing squadron. Even French and Spanish men of war were of little threat now, though most of them gave battle in vain with no result other than being sent to the bottom.

Perhaps the reputation of the *Polaris* was already spoken in hatred. About all that separated the convoy from common pirates at this point was that they did not deliberately go *looking* for plunder, instead maintaining their steady northern course, and British vessels were allowed to go on their way unhindered. Neutrals were fair game however, which flew in the face of international and maritime law. This was not what Reeman was dreaming of when he signed up for the Navy, but what could he do?

And still they sailed north, and still no one ever died.

7.

One day Reeman was searching by lanthorn in the lowest levels of the frigate for a suspected leak when he looked up and found himself suddenly confronted by Kent.

'Ah, my sporting fellow, we meet again.'

'Get away from me,' snarled Reeman.

'Oh my dear, is that any way to speak to your old friend?'

'We were never friends.'

Among the common seamen it was the height of fashion to grow their hair long into a queue, to be plaited in the normal course of events but carefully separated and combed out every Sunday for prayers. Some officers wore their hair long as was the old fashion though others were adopting the new mode of cutting their hair short. Kent, however defied every social convention of sea and land and had taken to shaving his head completely, like the warlock. It said more clearly than anything else whose boy he was, where his true loyalties lay. Now that they were assigned to the same ship Kent had resumed his lessons with the warlock openly, while still meeting all his regular shipboard duties and seeming to go days without sleep – more of the self-styled magician's ungodly training no doubt. Now, in the dimness below decks, Kent had taken off his cocked hat and his bald head shone dimly in the lanthorn's light.

'Did you want anything? Some of us have duties to attend to.'

'My dear, you must have been wondering what has been going on.'

'I wonder about nothing. I only care about being a King's officer.'

'You're a *good* boy,' sneered Kent, patting Reeman's head like a dog. 'Do you seriously mean you've had no curiosity at all about our mission?'

'No,' snapped Reeman, determined not to give the other passed midshipman any satisfaction.

'Well I'm going to tell you anyway. It will save me time, I think.

'The Admiralty were most impressed by the magister when he approached them. Once the most hated and feared man of society, he became a big-time hit with their lordships. Mr Nemo even boasts that he did not have to use his powers of influence, so impressed were they with his plan.

'The Magister has found a way to draw power from the magnetic field of the earth. The Admiralty assigned their top surgeon and scientific agent – who, of course, has many other functions – to Mr Nemo who before long vouched fully for his powers and learned how to benefit from the power of magnetism also. Nemo and Wolfe proposed to the Admiralty that the closer to north they were able to reach, the greater would be this effect. Wolfe also promised that he could devise a ritual that, performed close to magnetic north, would grant him overwhelming power which would enable him to defeat Napoleon quickly and easily with no further loss of resources. Their lordships gave their enthusiastic approval to this plan and granted them a state of the art cutter for northward travel as fast as possible, along with a surfeit of its top officers and men in the full knowledge that they could easily capture other vessels and their complements of crew and bring them under their influence. Does it gall you Reeman to know that the Admiralty have granted their full approval to everything that has happened here?'

'Why are you telling me about this?'

'Because you can do nothing about it. Nothing at all. And I know how much it hurts.' Kent turned abruptly on his heel and left, leaving Reeman with dark thoughts.

## 8.

The weather became increasingly cold.

Reeman started to wear greater numbers of layers from the slop chest beneath his uniform, and was at least gratified to notice that most of the other officers did so also, at least those still loyal to the British crown. Icebergs became increasingly common and more and more vigilance was required to avoid them. They were of course still headed north with all that meant. Reeman had decided to close his mind to all the implications of what they were doing and just perform all his duties mechanically. His conversation with Forester and Kent over the wardroom table was polite but empty and meaningless (which was all the Navy required at the best of times) and for whatever reason Kent did not repeat his revelation about the mission again, either in front of Forester or to Reeman alone. Reeman did not imagine this was out of politeness, but in fact Kent seemed to go out of his way to avoid him and certainly didn't initiation conversation – which was entirely welcome.

Days went on in this fashion until there came looming out of the icebergs and fog a French ship of the line.

It wasn't clear what such a vast man of war was doing out here. It might be that news of the convoy's activities had reached the French navy and they had sent the powerful vessel to intercept, though more likely it was in the north for some other reason. Whatever that might be there was only one course of action, and only one possible outcome at this point. While a ship of the line might be twice as powerful as a frigate with twice the number of gun decks or more, it still possessed only three masts and could not mount that much more sail. This made it much slower and far less manoeuvrable, particularly surrounded by icebergs, and it soon became clear that her captain was far less adept at navigating them than the British officers. It was also the case that any sailing vessel was vulnerable to attacks at the prow and stern;

and with the frigate giving battle from the front, the cutter and brig from the rear, and the lesser vessels swarming like ants and being treated as outright cannon fodder in most cases the *Rousseau* was soon captured. This gave Reeman no pleasure any longer, an experience he never thought he would know.

It was announced that Commander Forester would be taking over the *Rousseau*, with Commander Robinson being granted the *Cervantes* and Reeman and Kent being promoted to Acting Lieutenant to assist aboard the ship of the line. This was a moment Reeman had waited for all of his life, but at this point it was a hollow victory. What was genuinely baffling though, for all that Reeman now felt dead inside, was that the post captain would not be commanding the *Rousseau*. No lesser rank could possibly take possession of a line of battle ship. And for all that it was obvious what two men were really in overall command of the squadron, some lip service had to be paid to naval procedure, surely? In fact Captain O'Brian had not been seen throughout the battle; usually he had made sure to be prominently visible at the stern of the cutter, wearing full uniform and standing tall, the least a captain could do to keep up the morale of the crew.

It so happened that the surgeon was stood near to Reeman where he ruminated on the deck.

'Do you know,' Wolfe announced, 'I seem to recall I had something packed in my bag for just this sort of eventuality.' He reached down and rummaged in his doctor's portmanteau. 'Ah, here it is.' He pulled out a piece of cloth which he held by the corners and allowed the wind to shake out with a flourish. Reeman just about managed to prevent himself from groaning audibly. It was the broad pennant of a Commodore.

'What have we here,' chuckled the warlock. Reeman shook his head. Such was the esteem in which the Admiralty held their agent that they would grant him a rank exceeding that of a post captain.

*God help us all*, thought Reeman.

The flotilla carried on north, and a rumour began to circulate that Captain O'Brian was ill.

9.

Time passed.

The flotilla headed north, now somewhat slowed by
the addition of a line of battle ship – now a
Commodore's flagship, of course. Nemo and Wolfe
could now be seen on the *Rousseau's* quarterdeck
more often than not, arms folded and looking
smug. The warlock now led regular classes on the
foremast deck, teaching all who would attend his
bizarre movement regimes; advanced students such
as Kent would stand for hours in some of the most
awkward looking positions imaginable. Reeman
preferred to escape these by climbing up as high in
the rigging as possible, at least when the duties of
an Acting Lieutenant allowed him; these were so
onerous they almost enabled him to forget the
awful situation he was in, how much he hated it.
The surgeon seemed quite au fait with the duties of
a Commodore; on top of all his other talents, clearly
the Admiralty had had far more use for him than
just a surgeon. This did not stop the tortured
screams from the forbidden zones containing the

recusants, or the endless flow of wounded men returning to the crew pleased as Punch with increasingly horrible enhancements.

And still no one ever died despite that any ship of the line might feasibly expect to lose one man a month to accidents, and a squadron this size might double or triple that. But Captain O'Brian had never again been seen, and rumours of his illness became increasingly virulent.

Then one day a message came that the post captain wished to see Reeman about the *Polaris.*

Reeman had been so consumed by despair these past weeks he thought that he had become numb, but with this summons a new feeling came to him, that his heart was being squeezed in an iron gauntlet, a physical pain. What could the captain want with him after all this time, now that the squadron was in the grip of the most evil man who ever lived and the Admiralty's trusted agent? It was a long row from the *Rousseau* to the *Polaris,* and Reeman stood upright in the prow the entire time, boat cloak wrapped tight around him, wearing his cocked hat, heedless of the freezing spray. What did it matter anymore?

O'Brian was still in the same tiny cabin he had occupied at the beginning, but even within it he still looked small. He was lying back in his cot looking frail and old. His hair had evidently not been cut since the start of the mission, and what had once been short and iron grey now was long, sparse and wispy lying against the pillow. He had been aged from the beginning, but now looked ancient, as though he had endured fifty years. O'Brian opened watery eyes weakly and gazed at the midshipman.

Reeman,' he whispered. 'Thank God you came.'

Captain O'Brian, sir. You look... well.'

You're a terrible liar, Reeman.' They were alone in the cabin. The uniquitous Marine stood guard outside.

'I imagine rumours of my sickness have been all round the squadron.'

'Well...'

'We both know how impossible it is to keep information secret aboard Navy ships. Reeman, you're the only person I can talk to who knows how the King's navy should be. Not this abomination it has become.'

Reeman could only bow his head, face twisted in agony. The captain closed his eyes, breathing heavily for a while. Reeman wondered if he had fallen asleep, but O'Brian's eyes opened again.

'You're a good boy, Reeman.' The midshipman grimaced, being reminded of Kent's mocking words, but turned his face away so O'Brian wouldn't see this; he was sure the post-captain was sincere. 'I'm sorry I had to punish you that time. I'm sure you understand.'

'It was my fault, sir. I was in the wrong and you were in the right.'

'On the contrary, you were in the right for calling out that little turd. I should have clapped you on the shoulder, shaken your hand and loaded the pistols myself, but a King's captain can't be seen to encourage such behaviour.' O'Brian coughed and grimaced. 'He's the warlock's boy now, a real nasty piece of work. I'd see him court martialled if I ever got back to England, but now that will never happen.'

'Don't say that, sir-'

'Don't interrupt me. I'm not leaving this cabin alive again.'

'Sorry sir.' Reeman swallowed. 'Have you seen the surgeon?'

The captain's watery eyes opened wide. 'That godless spy? He's worse than the warlock. There's the man who is evil and the man who encourages and abets it. Those pair deserve each other. And they snared Kent, damn them to hell.' O'Brian's eyes closed again.

'We're in hell already, sir.' Reeman whispered.

'Not quite.' O'Brian coughed, and coughed, and seemed unable to stop coughing for quite a while. Reeman held a cloth to his lips; when the fit was over it was soaked with bright blood. 'I never bent the knee to that ungodly witch, never let that science agent near me. I've lived too long and will die my natural death as God intended. You're still pure too Reeman. Look over there, in the corner. Wrapped in that leather. I want you to have it.'

Reeman unwrapped it and gasped. It was a sword, straight in the old style. It looked ancient and had Latin writing engraved on the blade. It had no gold ornamentation as befitted the weapon of a professional warrior, but was clearly a priceless family heirloom to O'Brian, the kind passed on from father to-

'Sir! I can't have this!'

'You can and will. Yes, I wanted my son to have it, but that will never happen now.'

Reeman drew in a breath, then sighed. 'Thank you sir. I don't know what to say.'

'It's all right, you don't have to say anything. It's enough that you have the sword, and that you have a good heart. The Japanese are said to have a symbol, or a saying – I never really understood this, their writing is apparently more like pictures – of heart under blade. You have the heart of a true and good warrior, You deserve this sword. May you always lead the right life of a King's officer.'

O'Brian's eyes closed and didn't open again, though he continued to breathe raggedly. Reeman held onto the sword and stood for a while, head bowed. Eventually he put his other hand against O'Brian's shoulder, left it there for a few moments. Then he left the cabin. The Marine sentry saluted him on the way out.

Reeman knew now what he had to do.

10.

O'Brian died a few days later and was buried with full military honours. To date it was the only funeral they had had aboard the squadron, though in all Reeman's previous service they had been a common occurrence.

Reeman kept O'Brian's sword. A blue water sailing ship was not a place where one could keep a long rigid object constantly attached to one's belt in the normal course of events, but Reeman made sure always to have the weapon stashed in a safe place and always to be aware of its whereabouts, and checked up on it as often as he could manage. He wore it as part of his dress uniform for Sunday services as was an Acting Lieutenant's right, and while this drew occasional glances no one asked him about it. Perhaps no one else had even known the post captain had it with him, thus no one knew what it was. Perhaps people considered it was his own family's heirloom sword, Reeman thought bitterly. Kent had obviously seen him wearing it because before long his Sunday dress uniform included a sword on his belt as well, one lavishly ornamented with gold and jewels, in appearance far more impressive than Reeman's. Of course it was no doubt acquired through gambling or other immoral means, even the warlock's mind-control, but Reeman now gave as little thought as he could force himself to manage to the traitor Kent.

The squadron kept heading north. Before long there were more icebergs than blue water to traverse, and there were no true nights any longer, just different levels of sunlight. Reeman had slept badly before he received the post-captain's sword, but now he had it and his path was set his rest was undisturbed and the midnight sun didn't bother him. He would never return alive.

The speed of the squadron slowed as the ice increased, and the floating mountains posed more and more danger to the vessels. Eventually it was declared that they had penetrated close enough to magnetic north to enact the warlock's ritual. It was given out that to maximise its power as many people as possible had to witness it, and thus in stark defiance of all maritime safety the command was given out for the whole flotilla to be lashed together, to maximise the visibility of the warlock aboard the *Rousseau's* quarterdeck; all available hands would watch in the same manner as they witnessed punishment. This suited Reeman fine; he was determined that no one should get back to England to ever report what had happened here.

The long task of immobilising the vessels in a group was finally finished, and the grey light that passed for night was at its height. Nemo, clad in one of his most idiotic and pretentious robes, ascended grandly to the quarterdeck followed by a smirking Wolfe, whose commodore's pennant still flew at the masthead of the *Rousseau*. The men were crammed on every available deck space of all the vessels, shoulder to shoulder; even now the whole squadron was still heavily overmanned. Everyone stared raptly at the warlock as he raised his arms, gazed into the sky and started bellowing in some dreadful language. Reeman started forcing his way through the crowd to the hatch leading below. He didn't want to see this. Ordinarily the Marines would prevent any man leaving the deck at such a time, but as a trusted Acting Lieutenant, considered one of the most promising young men in the Navy, Reeman was allowed to go down.

He wasted no time in hurrying to the wardroom and armed himself with as much as he could carry. He had already made sure to fully load and check two repeaters and two conventional flintlock pistols before this all began; now, he stuck them in various pockets and belts all over his body. He buckled on his midshipman's dirk – though it was probably not much use to him now he wanted to remind himself of his duty and the time when he was once an idealistic young adolescent with no other dream than to command a King's ship. Finally, he strapped about himself the scabbard of the O'Brian family heirloom. Before he sheathed the blade he raised the hilt to his lips and kissed it. 'I won't fail you Captain,' he whispered. He was armed too heavily for any conventional naval battle and would probably sink straight to the bottom if he fell in, but he knew he would never leave this ship of the line again.

Now there was nothing left to do but make his way to the ship's magazine.

In accordance with the warlock's instructions that all available hands had to witness his ritual there was only a single Marine guarding the powder store, where gunpowder was stored in the enormously dangerous conditions which were most of the reason naked flames were banned below decks on any vessel. The Marine saluted and came to attention as Reeman approached. 'Sir!'

Reeman saluted back. 'Sergeant.' Reeman stared down the corridor as though trying to put his thoughts in order. 'I have a request from Commander Robinson. He wants you to report to-'

With shocking suddenness Reeman pulled his midshipman's dirk from behind his back where he had held it concealed and stabbed it up beneath the Marine's ribs into his heart. The sergeant died with a gurgle and a look of surprise. The midshipman felt sick, both nauseous to his stomach and sick at heart. He had been in plenty of battles and struck many blows in anger, but this was the first time he had murdered an innocent man in cold blood. He told himself it was for the greater good and that both himself and the Marine would soon be dead anyway, but he knew that if anything made it clear that his old life was gone forever, it was this day's work. Still, he would find validation and redemption soon enough. He hoped.

Reeman opened the powder store, stepped inside and gazed about. He took out a long piece of quick match he had secured earlier – string soaked in wet inflammable material and allowed to dry that would burn along its length faster than any man could prevent – opened a couple of barrels and strewed their deadly contents on the floor, and made sure one end of the match was well located, fixed and tied in several places in the black powder now scattered all about. He then paused.

Reeman had realised a while back that the most pragmatic, expedient and sensible course of action, the one most likely to succeed, was just to fire the powder right now and not bother with the quick match and the rest of his plan. With what he intended there were any number of things that could go wrong; better to take the safe route perhaps.

But Reeman had taken O'Brian's words to heart about his ancestral sword, the Japanese motto of the heart under blade. He had decided that a King's officer didn't always do the safest, most pragmatic thing; he did the *right* thing. Reeman would like to live up to the post-captain's words. He wanted to do the right thing.

And he wanted most dearly to do what he was about to do.

Reeman tied the other end of the quick match to his belt and made his way back through the deserted lower decks. He chose a route which would take him directly to the quarterdeck, checking every so often that the length of quick match hadn't got caught. At last he arrived, immediately below where he wanted to be. He took a deep breath, composed himself and made his final preparations. He threw open the hatch and started up.

Even the grey light above was bright after the dimness below decks. The warlock was still bellowing his ungodly words, careless of what was going on about him. The surgeon though looked down and saw Reeman emerging from below. Wolfe frowned and with a look of annoyance opened his mouth to berate the midshipman, but when he saw the intent in Reeman's eyes his expression changed to alarm and he tried to shout a warning. Too late.

Still with his legs below decks Reeman pulled out a repeater pistol in each hand. With one shot he gunned down the warlock and with the other he slew the surgeon. Whatever evil powers Nemo and Wolfe might have tapped into between them, at this last hour it didn't protect either of them from a ball of hot lead straight through the skull. Both men died immediately. Reeman had always been a good shot.

Then all hell broke loose.

Several things happened at once. Immediately throughout the flotilla, as soon as the warlock was slain every one of the unearthly prosthetics the wounded men had been fitted with ceased to function. The light went out in Mr Midshipman Mills' glass eye in the bronze half of his skull and in his human eye as well. His young life ended now for real. His jaw fell slack, he collapsed to his knees and over on to his face. The glass eye shattered and a wisp of smoke dissipated away with an agonised, barely-audible scream of its own. The man whose lung had been replaced by canvas abruptly screamed in terrible agony, clutching that side of his body. 'IT HURTS! IT HURTS! OH, MOTHER OF GOD!' He too collapsed, writhing around on the deck, shrieking and shrieking.

Many of the other men had had articulated limbs fitted made of metal; these too ceased to work. A few were incapacitated by sudden agony and fell, but others found that they had large, heavy and now immobile hunks of material attached to themselves which were of little or no use. In a few cases this was automatically fatal as they were no longer able to cling to the rigging or the rails and fell into the sea; dragged down by the extra mass, they perished in the ice-filled waters. For others the prosthetics weighed them down to the point they were unable to move; they dropped or were immobilised in place.

But many more found that the prosthetics served perfectly well as slashing, bludgeoning and piercing weapons in their own right, and absolutely all of the men who owed allegiance to the warlock and surgeon – which was more than two-thirds of the entire squadron by this point – were maddened with rage at the sight of their liege-lord's slaying and fought with a fury which could have come straight from the Devil himself. Reeman was gratified to see that most of the King's commissioned and warrant officers still fought on the side of untainted humanity, as did many of the French and Spanish trusted men; but they were well in the minority. Reeman and everyone else were fighting for their lives.

The battle would have been won by the warlock's furious followers except for the fact that the Satanic anger animating them seemed to soon fade away. Those that had cheated death found that it caught up with them as whatever power keeping them going failed. Before long men began to drop like flies, and even those who had survived the failure of their prosthetic limbs collapsed and died. But by this point most had had chance to inflict on those who were still loyal grievous and fatal injuries. Reeman soon found himself alone on the quarterdeck, bleeding from a dozen wounds, many serious. Only his youth and strength, and the fact that he had prepared for the battle by getting armed to the teeth, had preserved him this long. He looked around wildly, looking for life on the decks all about, seeing nothing but broken and dying men. For a moment he let himself think that it was all over, that he had solved everything and saved the day, that he might still get out of this alive-

Then a slender blade slipped into his bowels from behind.

Reeman gasped in agony and collapsed forward. With the self-preservation instinct of a seasoned fighter he wouldn't let himself surrender to pain, but rolled over and threw himself to his feet. He grabbed for a weapon only to remember that all his pistols, the repeaters and the flintlocks, had been exhausted of ammunition and hurled at enemies. His hand closed about the hilt of O'Brian's sword, his last hope.

Facing him was Kent.

'Filthy bastard!' the traitor spat. 'The magister would have brought us power overwhelming! And you killed him.'

'Your domination of evil is over, Kent,' Reeman gasped. He had clutched his hand to his stomach where he was bleeding heavily both from the entry point of Kent's valuable sword into his back and his front where the tip had emerged, doing more damage. He was in sufficient agony that he knew his intestines had been pierced, an automatic death sentence. Still there was some chance. There always was for a King's officer.

'That's what you think. The Master has taught me more than enough to complete his ritual. Soon all that power will be mine, and all your stupidity will have been for nothing.' Kent had lost his cocked hat (or never bothered wearing it) and his bald head shone obscenely in the grey light. He appeared lightly wounded if at all.

'Not if I kill you.'

'You are welcome to try! But enough talk! Have at you!' Mouth twisted in a sneer, Kent stepped back and drew himself upright. He raised his valuable sword up in a perfect fencing salute, executed a flourish and dropped into a clearly very well practised ready stance.

Reeman had no idea what any of this was and he had already been badly wounded before Kent had stabbed him in the back. He managed to draw O'Brian's sword and kissed the hilt again. 'I won't fail you Captain,' he whispered, and pointed the tip at Kent.

The other midshipman lunged and stabbed him through the lung before Reeman could even react.

It became rapidly clear that on top of all his other talents and despicable nature Kent was a champion fencer. With the warlock's apprentice lancing effortlessly through Reeman's clumsy attempts to block or parry, the loyal midshipman's lungs were soon both filling with blood and Kent had pierced his liver and kidneys as accurately and easily as if he were demonstrating an anatomy diagram. Reeman spat blood. 'Why don't you just kill me?'

'What would be the fun in that?' Kent lunged again and stabbed Reeman through the swordarm, then twisted the blade viciously. O'Brian's heirloom sword fell from suddenly nerveless fingers. Reeman groped for his midshipman's dirk with his other hand, but even that was gone. 'Forgive me Captain,' he whispered. 'I have failed you.'

'That you have. And yet, as an exercise of my new powers, I think I shall keep you alive to look upon all I shall achieve when the Magister's power is mine.'

Reeman knew that all hope was gone and he faced a fate worse than death. For one despairing moment he thought of throwing himself over the side just so he wouldn't have to witness Kent's empowerment and victory.

Then he smelled smoke.

With his last strength Reeman looked around, searching for the source. Down on a lower deck he saw that a fire had broken out in some tarred rigging, no doubt ignited by a firearm discharge earlier in the battle. This currently small flame would rapidly become a serious problem for anyone left alive aboard ship, but Reeman was now determined that there wouldn't be anyone left to be worried about fire.

He knew what he had to do.

'A King's officer always does his duty,' he said, and threw himself backwards off the quarterdeck. He had aimed right, and fell directly on top of the burning rigging. The flame was as yet too small to burn him through his clothes, but far more painful was the impact which broke his bones and mauled him. Still, this was of no concern any longer.

It was not until now that Kent finally noticed the length of quick match which had remained tied to Reeman's belt all this time.

'What?' gasped the warlock's apprentice. 'No!' He stared in horror at the inflammable line leading below, only now realising what it must mean. Reeman smiled.

The fire was still small but it was enough to ignite quick match. The flame caught and raced down quicker than any man could prevent. It ran into the scattered black powder below decks and fired the entire magazine store of the ship of the line. The vessel exploded and smashed the whole lashed-together squadron to matchwood. Reeman and

Kent were close enough to the blast to be atomised. Their two swords were blasted in opposite directions and found their long homes on the icy seabed of the Arctic. In the end Kent's valuable sword had done him no good, but the O'Brian family heirloom had fulfilled its destiny.

# EPILOGUE

It was not in fact the case that no one remained alive to get back to England and tell the tale of what had happened here, though that had been Reeman's original intention. Even after the biggest explosion something remains, and after the squadron's demise there was plenty of floating wreckage a sailor could cling to, even a couple of small boats left. A few men managed to survive the battle, the blast and the freezing waters, and it was subsequently not impossible to get back to civilisation.

However, all that they could do was tell their crazy, terrifying story in quayside taverns or in the messes of whatever new vessels they found themselves in. It was very easy for their audiences to dismiss it all as tall seamen's tales, and in time it was easy for even those who had been there to doubt the veracity of events as well. Warlocks and evil powers were the stuff of legend; surely none of it really happened? It was easier and more productive to write it all off and return to the life of an honest seaman, and the survivors were happier for it.

If any of these rumours or stories ever got back to the Admiralty they made no official comment. It could not be ignored that a state of the art cutter and a large complement of the Navy's best officers and men had been lost forever, but as the Napoleonic wars raged on it was easy enough to write them off to enemy action. There are however no official records that the British military tried again to enlist the forces of occultism, magick or witchcraft....

.. Except that by the nineteen forties a new conflict had arisen, against an enemy whom dread rumour held responsible for using their own evil, twisted version of magick, and who used as their symbol an ancient Eastern sign originally representing the sun but here reversed so it attracted evil energies and not good. So in this new war a man in British Intelligence called Maxwell Knight founded a group called Night's Black Agents, and he conversed with a man named Dennis Wheatley, who had met a man who was once known as Edward Alexander...

But that's another story.

Printed in Great Britain
by Amazon

41865825R00069